For anyone who has looked at a wall and seen a canvas instead — VV

To my bashert — AP

Text copyright © 2021 by Vikki VanSickle
Illustrations copyright © 2021 by Anna Pirolli
Illustrations published by arrangement with Debbie Bibo Agency

Tundra Books, an imprint of Penguin Random House Canada Young Readers,
a division of Penguin Random House of Canada Limited

Library and Archives Canada Cataloguing in Publication

Title: Anonymouse / Vikki VanSickle ; {illustrations by} Anna Pirolli.
Names: VanSickle, Vikki, 1982- author. | Pirolli, Anna, illustrator.
Identifiers: Canadiana (print) 20200177702 | Canadiana (ebook) 20200177710 |
ISBN 9780735263949 (hardcover) | ISBN 9780735263956 (EPUB)
Classification: LCC PS8643.A59 A76 2021 | DDC jC813/.6-dc23

Published simultaneously in the United States of America by Tundra Books of Northern New York,
an imprint of Penguin Random House Canada Young Readers, a division of Penguin Random House of Canada Limited

Library of Congress Control Number: 2020931171

Edited by Samantha Swenson
Designed by John Martz
The artwork in this book was rendered digitally.
The text was set in P22 Mayflower.

Printed and bound in China

www.penguinrandomhouse.ca

2 3 4 5   25 24 23 22 21

Penguin
Random House
TUNDRA BOOKS

Anonymouse

WORDS BY   PICTURES BY

Vikki VanSickle   Anna Pirolli

tundra

One morning a tired city rat made her way home.

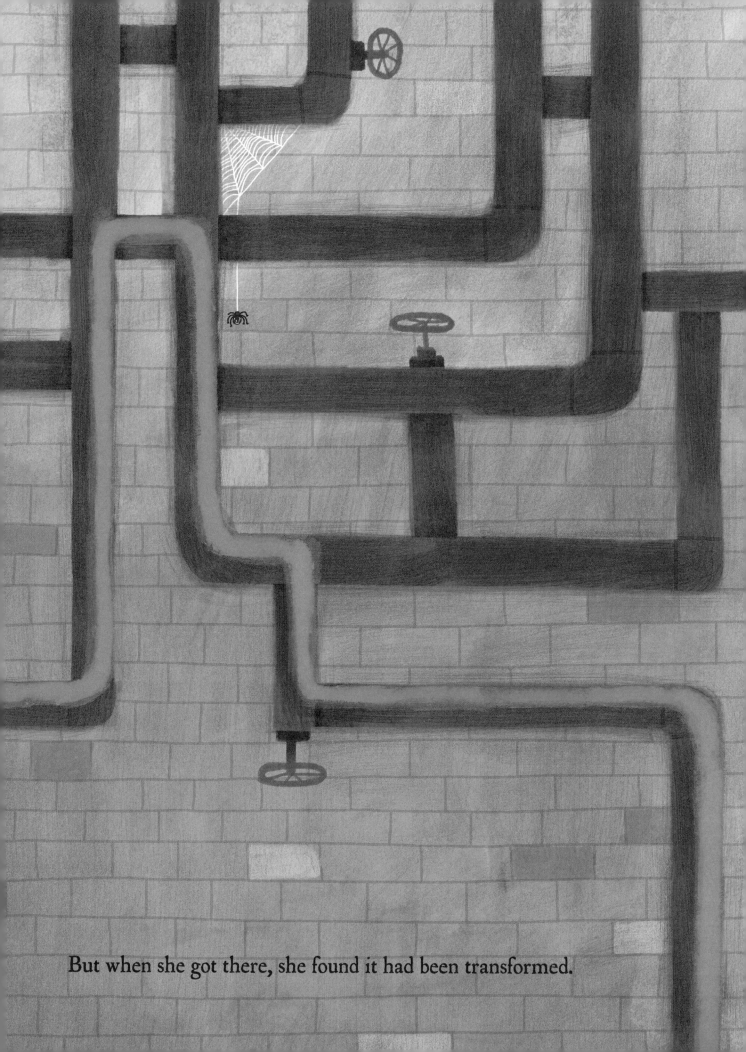

But when she got there, she found it had been transformed.

Across the city a colony of bats was settling
in for a good day's sleep, when they
noticed something unusual . . .

. . . very unusual. There was no explanation, only a name.

Anonymouse

Suddenly, Anonymouse's art was everywhere.

No canvas was too high.

Or too low.

Or too unusual.

Sometimes it was funny.

Sometimes it was serious.

But it always made the animals of the city think.

Time went by.
The art faded, became obscured
or disappeared completely.

There hadn't been anything new from
Anonymouse in a long time.

The animals of the city missed Anonymouse's perspective.
They worried that something bad had happened.

After all, the city can be dangerous for animals.

More time went by, with no sign of Anonymouse.

But his art left a lasting impression on the animals of the city.

Thanks to Anonymouse, they looked at the city in a whole new way.

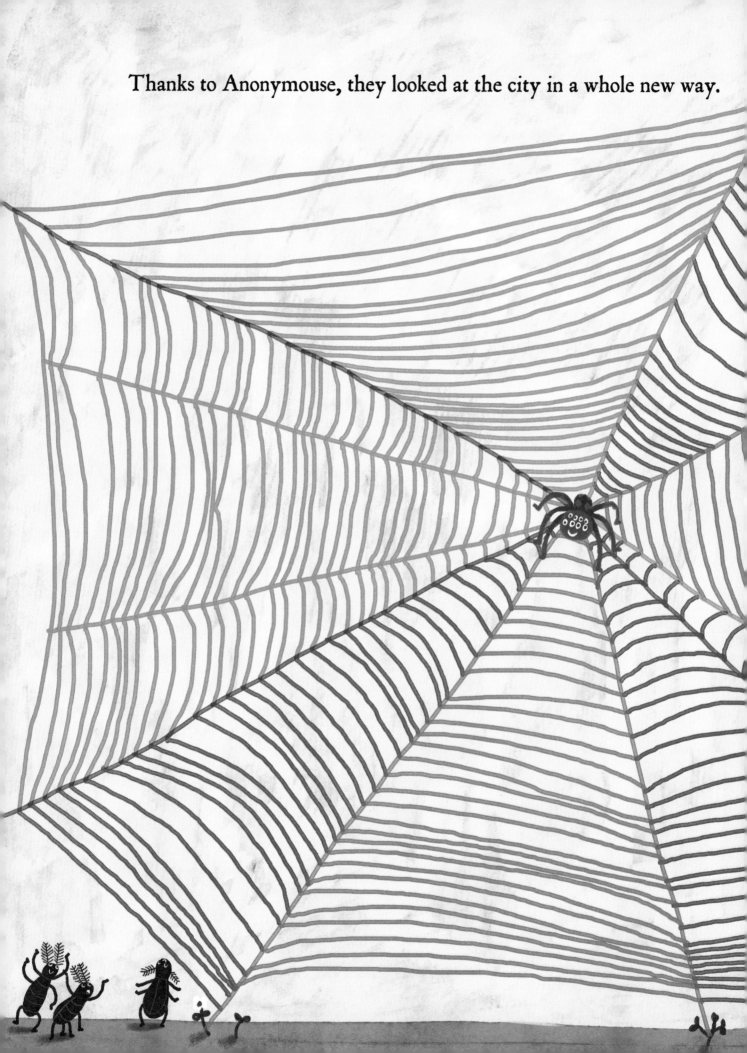

As for Anonymouse?

The world is his canvas.